MEDIUM BOILED

Thomson Burtis

Pharos Books

ISBN: 978-93-67007-21-1
eISBN: 978-93-59839-40-0

©Publishers

Publisher: Pharos Books (P) Ltd.
Plot No.-63, First Floor, Main Mother Dairy Road
Pandav Nagar, East Delhi-110092
Phone: +14049995474, 011-40395855
WhatsApp: +91 9319228272
E-mail: sales@pharosbooks.in
Website: www.pharosbooks.in
Edition: 2024

Printed By: Sushma Book Binding House, Okhla
Industrial Area, Phase II, New Delhi-110020

Medium Boiled
By : Thomson Burtis

Medium Boiled

Storm flight with the Border Air Patrol

The big De Haviland bombing plane was a little more than eight thousand feet high, and "Shag" Moran, its pilot, had an excellent view of a considerable portion of south Texas. His big body was hunched deep into the front cockpit to avoid the terrific airblast which swept back from the propeller, and his black eyes alternated the maze of unfamiliar instruments before him and the unending desert of mesquite below. In long, gray-green waves the chaparral billowed away to the horizon on every side, and there was not so much as a wisp of smoke to indicate that a living thing inhabitated that trackless waste, a mile and a half below.

It was a sight calculated to make any pilot concentrate on his motor, for there was no possible landing field below, in case that twelve-cylinder Liberty ahead should start to miss. To Shag Moran, however, the very ugliness and desolation of it was a pleasant thrill—a constant reminder of where he was going, and why. Even the thought of himself, alone in a world of his own, was delightful, for the time being. It was the visible evidence of the fact that he had attained combined objectives for which he had dared not hope, three months before.

"First Lieutenant John Moran, of the McMullen flight of the Border patrol—" He mouthed the words with leaping heart us his eyes swept the wastes below him, which seemed to epitomize all the romance and danger of the job he was on his way to do. He was bound for the border. More than that, he was to be a member of the blue ribbon outfit of the Army Air Service, the Border patrol. And as the last ingredient of what he conceived to be flyer's paradise, he was to be one of the McMullen flight of that patrol—the flight with the finest record along the Rio Grande.

The miracle—for miracle it was—was still unreal to him. Of course, they were ordering extra men to the patrol. The underground gossip, which was running like wildfire through the Air Service, was that ? was due to pop along the Border. The smuggling in of aliens had reached tremendous proportions, and the guarded conversation of higher offices was to the effect that one of the largest, nerviest and wealthiest rings which had ever operated in Texas was due for a roundup.

But that Shag Moran had been picked to go to the patrol was purely a mistake. Moran admitted that. Some slip-up in Washington. Why, he'd only got his wings a few short weeks before, and had scarcely two hundred hours in the air. Not enough experience for border service, he reflected. But he'd bluff it through, and cut out his tongue before he let anyone know what an amateur he was. And he'd fly with any of them.

He grinned to himself as he thought:

"Boy, what they'd say if they knew that I never flew a De Haviland in my life before today! But I got this baby off the ground at Donovan and nobody'll ever dream I never flew one!"

No more than they'd dream how much his wings and flying meant to him. The dogged, heart-breaking fight he had waged to drag himself from the poverty-stricken slime of his boyhood, through school, and then to an officer's commission. The ambition of terrible years was fulfilled for Shag Moran. And nobody suspected that there had been tears in his eyes when he got his commission. Big, hulking, shambling Shag Moran was supposed to be hard-boiled. That's what the carelessly competent young fliers thought about him, and he was glad of it. He would have cut off his hand rather than let them know his real love for the air, and of his perfect contentment, now that he was a flyer. Why, if the border men knew how he felt about being one of them, they'd laugh themselves sick. Think he was crazy. They took the job as a matter of course. They hadn't worked a lifetime for it.

There was McMullen, and he was going to hit it right on the nose. It must be, according to his map. There was a dun pocket-handkerchief of a field, surrounded by buildings, a few miles west of a sizable town. Surely those big, black blotches against the ground were the two iron hangars flanking the field to east and west. And that town was McMullen, all right—it was too big to be an unnoted settlement. Southward a few miles the Rio Grande was a twisting, silver ribbon, glinting in the flooding sunlight.

He'd start down, now. Had he been more familiar with De Havilands, he might have essayed spiraling down closer to the field. He would take no chances now, though.

He eased back on the throttle, until the tachometer was down to nine hundred revolutions a minute, and nosed down slowly. He watched his airspeed meter like a hawk. He kept the speed of his ship at a hundred miles an hour. The wind was making the wires sing, and there was considerable vibration.

In a perfectly straight, conservative dive he flashed earthward, his body tense with the strain. Now he could see tiny figures lounging on the steps of one of the buildings which formed the southern boundary of the sandy airdrome. He was going to have an audience for his landing, which made it worse. With every moment, it seemed, that field was shrinking in size. The northern boundary of it was a fence. He prayed that the wind would be from the south, so that he could land in from the north. It would be impossible for him to bring that big plane down over the obstacles on the other three sides.

The altimeter read a thousand feet when he pulled the ship up and shoved the gun all the way on. He was a half mile back of the field as he flew level toward it. He circled it once, and saw that the wind-sausage on top of one of the corrugated iron hangars indicated a south-east wind. Some one had said that the wind was usually southeast—the Gulf breeze. Yes, there were at least a half dozen men lounging in the shade of a porch. There were several buildings along that southern rim, and two long lines of tents.

He drove northward a half mile, circled warily, and cut the gun to seven hundred revolutions. He fairly felt his way toward the ground, trying to watch the ground, his airspeed and the tachometer all at once. He must barely ease over that fence, at the lowest speed possible.

He got too low. He was only fifty feet high, several hundred yards back of the fence, and the motor barked into sudden life as his hand thrust the throttle forward. He seemed to be going terribly fast, for being so close to the fence, and he cut the motor to idling. Downward, bit by bit, the fence had flashed beneath him. He was going like lightning.

From a height of six feet it seemed that the D.H. dropped out from underneath him. The wheels hit the ground hard, and the big ship bounced high in the air. His hand automatically found the throttle as the plane hung, nose in the air, and jammed it all the way forward.

He'd have to go around again. Cursing himself for a clumsy fool, he raved—

"I thought I was flying a Jenny, ? it! I ought to be pushing baby carriages."

Those veterans down there were laughing at him, doubtlessly. Having to go around twice to make a field—an airdrome—with a perfectly good motor. He had looked like a cadet, on his first solo.

Again he shot for the field and this time, with his heart in his mouth, he got to a foot above the ground with the fence only twenty-five feet behind him, and he held the ship there. Again it seemed that he was going at express-train speed, but he caught the drop in time. He jerked the stick back, and although he was a bit late, the ship only bounced once, and scarcely more than a foot. The buildings seemed a safe distance ahead, too.

They were, for a Jenny, but not for a heavy D.H., rolling fast on a hard, sand field as smooth as a floor. Desperately he cut the switches, and finally, panic-stricken, threw his stick to one side and jammed on full rudder. The D.H. ground-looped, one wing-skid dragging the ground. Not enough to cause any damage, though, and as he snapped on the switches again he told himself:

"I got down—but how? This time I was going too ? fast, after coming in too slow the first time."

Mechanics were waving him toward the line in front of the eastern hangars, and he taxied toward them, gingerly. He felt that he was handling the D.H. awkwardly. It was infinitely more responsive, even on the ground, than a Jenny. Somehow or other he felt uncertain, now, about his ability to control these bigger ships as he had learned to master the training planes.

He was grateful for the fact that the mechanics came out to meet him, and by pulling on the wingtips helped him, into the line straight. At the same time his quick sensitiveness made him wonder whether they were doing it because they had noticed his uncertainy in handling his ship.

A short, stocky officer was coming toward him, and on the collar of his O.D. shirt were the bars of a captain. That was the famous Captain Kennard—two planes to his credit in France, D.S.C. and Croix De Guerre, recognized as the best squadron commander on the border.

Moran came to attention, and the square-faced captain returned his salute nonchalantly.

"You're Moran, eh?" he said in a raucous voice, and his face, scarred by innumerable wrecks, split into a genial grin. "Glad to see you. The boys'll unwire your suitcase. Come on over and meet the gang."

Moran relaxed a bit. So the C.O. wasn't going to hop on him about that landing right away, he reflected gratefully. He removed his helmet in the withering heat, baring the coarse, unruly black hair which had given him his nickname. Perhaps his beard had had something to do with it, too. Sometimes he shaved twice a day in an endeavor to control it, but his heavy jaw always looked dark and bristly, nevertheless.

"Sure glad to see you," repeated Kennard, his bowed legs moving faster than Moran's unusually long ones. "They're flying us ragged, and a new man's welcome."

"I heard something was up, but no one seemed to know much about it," ventured Moran.

"We don't know a ? of a lot, ourselves," Kennard told him. "But it's pretty plain that they're watching a gang in Mexico who've been running chinks and other immigrants over. The runners get around a thousand per man, delivered in San Antone. Army of 'em. Anyway, it's patrol all day, and be on the alert all night, with a dozen false alarms every hour. Must be good and big and tough, this gang, or Washington wouldn't be acting as though there was a war on.

"Attention, boys and girls. Here's the latest victim. Moran, shake hands with Tex MacDowell, Slim Evans, Pop Cravath, George Hickman, and last, but not least, Dumpy Scarth."

Moran recognized all but the last man from things he'd heard about them. Lean, lounging "Tex" MacDowell; "Slim" Evans, who was nearly six feet six inches tall and as thin as a rail; big, blond Hickman and "Pop" Cravath, who were observers.

"Dumpy" Scarth was a new name to him, and he had thought he knew every member of the flight by name and description. Scarth was a short, fat, little fellow, with a pug nose, a full moon-face, and boyish eyes, which looked the big, new man over with a critical air.

"I know of all of you," Moran told them slowly. "That is, except Scarth here. I—er—never heard—"

"He just joined the outfit," Kennard informed him.

"Then you're new to the border too?" Moran said awkwardly. He was in an agony of self-consciousness, because of the figure he'd cut on that landing.

"What?" squawked Scarth. "New to the border! Why, I've been with the Laredo flight for years! Didn't you ever hear of that Caloras case?"

"No, probably he didn't," Slim Evans cut in casually. "There really are a few birds in the world who've never heard of you, Dumpy."

Scarth bridled like a bantam rooster. Now he looked Moran over scornfully, and Shag was suddenly aware that his shoes were wrinkled and unpolished and clumsy looking. Kate, his sister and only surviving relative, cost him a good deal in college. Too much for him to afford forty dollar boots and hundred and fifty dollar uniforms.

"You sure came in in a burst of glory," Scarth informed him with relish. "Two bounces—I thought sure you were a major."

"I—er—hit an airpocket the first time," Moran told him.

He was standing at the foot of the steps, shifting from one foot to another, always conscious of the speculative scrutiny to which he was being subjected by the men who would have to live on intimate terms with him for months.

"Air pocket ?!" yapped Dumpy.

"You were coming in too slow! The second time you looked as though you were trying to break speed records. I suppose the wind shifted on your tail that time."

It had come. Suddenly Shag was conscious of an overweening desire to close Hearth's mouth for him. The others had said nothing.

"Not exactly," he said with difficulty, moistening his lips. He felt as if he was on trial. "The throttle stuck a minute, and the motor was turning up pretty fast—"

"Listen to Alibi Ike!" jeered Dumpy. "Had much time on D.H.'s?"

Moran's eyes were stormy, his heavy face set. ? this cocky, nasty little runt—

"Why," he began, moistening his lips, "I—"

"Dry up, Dumpy," drawled Tex MacDowell easily. "Likewise, lay off. What the ? are you catechizing about?"

"Hello, here comes Jimmy Jennings, and my ship's coming out. Come on, Pop!" Dumpy exclaimed, forgetting everything else.

He ran for his helmet and goggles as Moran watched the incoming patrolship enter the field. He knew who Jimmy Jennings was. A border veteran, and an ace.

The big D.H. roared across the airdrome, from the east, circled a hundred feet north of the field, and suddenly tilted on one wing. Down it came in a terrific sideslip, its nose parallel to the fence. Thirty feet above the ground it dived out of the slip, nose coming around toward the field, and as it came across the fence the pilot skidded it sidewise to kill speed.

Starting two hundred feet high, only a few yards back of the fence, the pilot had brought the ship to the ground as lightly as a feather, within twenty-five yards of the fence, and stopped rolling a little more than halfway across the field.

"That's flying," Shag thought humbly.

"Don't mind Dumpy," Slim Evans advised him spaciously. "Dumpy firmly believes he's the world's best flyer, frankly admits it on every provocation, and the ? of it is that he's ? near right!"

"What are you going to do with a man that brags all night, and then goes out and proves the next day that he can live up to his bragging?" grinned Kennard.

"Every new man is a prospective rival to him," Slim went on, "and he tries to put said rookie in his place. But he's a great little cuss when you get to know him—"

"Watch him prove something now."

Moran watched, and held his breath. Dumpy took off from the northern end of the field, cleared the buildings, and then turned back. He swooped low across the ground on his return trip, and then, for a full minute, he showed what could be done with a big bomber in the hands of a master. He chased his own tail like a gargantuan dragon fly, tipping the D.H. up into vertical banks in which the lower wingtip was only inches off the ground. One final rush across the field, another zoom in which the ship stood on its tail and appeared to climb up the side of the recreation building, and he was off.

"That's him, himself," grinned Hickman, who was almost as big as Moran. "You gave him an opening by springing those alibies."

"They weren't alibies—"

"The ? they weren't," Kennard advised him. "We listen to too many of 'em down here. This field's tough the first few times, and good flyers've ? near starved to death, they had to go around so many times. And every ? one with an alibi, instead of admitting it. Like you."

Hurt, Moran stiffened.

"Well, alibi or no alibi, that little squirt, Scarth, better not buzz around too much, kidding people he don't know," he said gruffly. "Captain, can I be shown to my tent to clean up?"

Kennard looked at him curiously for a moment before replying. The others, it seemed, had been taken aback by his rasping ultimatum. Then:

"You may. Orderly! Show Lieutenant Moran to Tent Six."

Vaguely miserable, Moran followed the orderly to the small, floored tent which was to be his border domicile. By the time he had set his things in order his trunk was brought from the afternoon train, and he was busy until six, straightening his meager effects and washing up in the bathhouse, down at the end of the boardwalk which ran between the two rows of tents. He was tying his tie when Slim Evans poked his long, thin nose into the tent.

"About chow time," he said cheerily.

"Come on over."

Moran, though grateful for Slim's interest, merely nodded, and in a moment joined him.

"By the way," Slim said casually, "if you like I'll go up with you tomorrow. There are some tricks about this field in this light air, and—"

"?, does one punk landing put me under instruction again? I've landed in worse fields than this one."

Slim looked at him, and Moran averted his face to hide what he felt was a telltale flush. He had been betrayed by his anxiety to hide the fact that he was a raw amateur who had no business on the border.

"As you please," the lanky airman said laconically, nor did he speak again until they entered the dining hall.

The others were already at the table, and a Chinaman was removing the soup plates.

"Jerry Sims and Tom Daly got it today— Just got a radiogram," barked Kennard from the head of the table.

"What?" yelped Slim. "How?"

"Must have been a forced landing in the fountains within a few miles of El Paso. In a cañon, crashed, burned."

"God Almighty."

The table had been quiet, Moran noticed, when they entered. Those tanned faces were set, and the eyes somehow old. Kennard directed his gaze to Moran.

"Know either one of 'em?" he inquired. "Marfa flight. They were great eggs."

Moran shook his head. The death toll of the border flyers totaled one out of eight, every year, he knew, and that very afternoon two of them had gone. In the mountains of the Big Bend.

He cleared his throat as he helped himself to bread. Because the simply told news affected him, he said bruskly—

"Well, that's what any man in this business has got to expect, and he can't kick when he kicks off."

"The ? he can't!"

It was stout, fiery Pop Cravath, his eyes snapping. Daly had been his friend.

"I suppose you look forward to burning to death, eh? Hard-boiled egg we have with us!" he stormed on.

Moran was in his shell, like a turtle. His eyes met Cravath's squarely as he stumbled on.

"Every man knows what to expect—it's just an incident—"

"You don't say! We'll give a dance in honor of it, I suppose, to let the world know that a few deaths here and there don't faze our nervy pilots!" Cravath spat bitterly. "I'm ? if I'm not sick of these guys that shoot off their mouths about how little danger means to them—when hard luck hits somebody else! And how loud they yelp when it hits them—"

"The worst of it is," Kennard slid in, "that we can't even go over into Mexico tonight, ? it!"

The object of his words had been to cut off the hot-tempered Cravath, Moran knew, and to ease the tension which had fallen over the depressed table.

The C.O.'s eyes were very keen and very cold as they rested on his newest flyer. He went on gruffly:

"It's the custom to go on a howling drunk every time a man gets knocked off and sort of forget it. Now we've got to stay on duty."

"They might have picked a better time to get killed, at that," Dumpy Scarth remarked.

Moran's eyes were on his plate. What had he said that they should disapprove of? Maybe he'd been a little rough for a newcomer. He'd just wanted to show them that he belonged. Why should they pick on him? Every move he made was a mistake, as far as they were concerned. Slowly, as he mulled it over in his mind, his misery congealed into resentment.

Always taciturn, he did not say a word during the remainder of the meal. Instinctively he felt that he wanted to be by himself, and he went directly to his tent. He lay there, thinking. Sensitive to the point of mania, he felt that he was off on the wrong foot with such speed that he could never start over again. His own fault, too. Trying to show off.

No, it wasn't. Why had that fat-headed runt, Scarth, started picking on him right away?

Toward midnight the flyers, who had been playing cards in the recreation room, came to their tents, and devil-may-care laughter died away into quiet. Shag lumbered to his feet, and went out into the starlit night. The mesquite was murmuring, crackling softly, in the Gulf breeze, and the sky was like a purple roof over him. Over at headquarters, guards were at the telephone, and lights gleamed in the radio shack. East and west stretched the border—hundreds of miles. Southward, Mexico was like a brooding desert. Somehow all the romance, all the tradition, all the pregnant possibilities of the Border country seemed to be whispering to him from the velvet darkness, and his big body thrilled to it and his eyes glowed.

His imagination leaped from station to station—Laredo, Del Rio, Sanderson, Marfa—and he could see the ships on the line, looming like crouching monsters in the darkness, ready to spring into the air after their prey. Life could hold nothing to compare with this, and he was a part of it.

No, he wasn't, he thought as he went to bed with a thousand thoughts rioting in his brain. But he would be.

Two ships were off on the dawn patrol when he ate breakfast next morning—Dumpy Scarth and Tex MacDowell, with their observers. The others greeted him more or less naturally, but he could see that he was already pegged in their minds as a queer egg. He tried to force himself out of his customary taciturnity but it was hard.

At the end of the meal he said to the captain—

"If it's all right, sir, I'd like to practise a few landings."

"Sure. Your ship'll be No. 8."

Moran dreaded the prospect of learning to land a D.H. on that field, but it had to be done. Why hadn't he been man enough to admit his ignorance of big ships, and practise landings up at Donovan?

He knew that the bombers were considered too frail to stunt, so he went on with assumed carelessness—

"Do you people down here live up to that 'no stunt' stuff on those babies?"

"Of course!" snapped Kennard. "We don't make a habit of slapping God in the face."

The others grinned, their eyes on Moran.

"Perhaps you twist 'em around regularly?" inquired Slim Evans, and Moran flushed.

"Just wanted to know," he said awkwardly, and went out.

Ten minutes later he was in the front cockpit of No. 8, trying out the already warm motor. A mechanic held each wingtip, another sat on the tail and leaned against the airblast as he covered his eyes from the dust which swirled upward in a dense, cone-shaped cloud. The tires strained against the wheelblocks as Moran held the throttle wide open, his eyes sweeping his instruments. Air pressure, three; battery charging rate, two; temperature, eight degrees Centigrade; tachometer showing, 1750; oil pressure, twenty-five—all was as it should be, as far as he knew. He turned off one switch of the double ignition system, and listened. Not a miss. Then a brief tryout of the other switch, and he eased the gun back to idling. He adjusted his goggles and nodded to the crew, with a lump in his throat.

They pulled the wheelblocks, and he taxied to the northern end of the field. He turned safely, and gave it the gun. He knew he could take off all right. Pressing forward on the stick, feet braced against the rudder, he sent his ship roaring across the field, nose low to the ground. It took the air by itself, almost, and he swept across the buildings with twenty-five feet to spare.

In the cool, smooth morning air he felt some of his confidence return, and when he felt his way down across the fence at a mere seventy-five miles an hour he was sure he was going to make the field. He dared a skid to kill more speed, after he had leveled off and, although he bounced, the ship came to earth safely and stopped rolling with a bare twenty-five feet to spare.

Five times he landed, and three times he made it on the first try. He still felt strange in it, and there was uncertainty in each landing. But he had self-confidence in the air, and there was no doubt now that eventually he'd be a capable De Haviland man even on that tiny field.

He decided to go high, and bank and sideslip and stall around a bit to get more accustomed to his ship. It was a thrill to feel the excess power in that motor. The air was pleasant to his perspiring face as it swept by him. He took in the view, avidly. McMullen, a small splotch on the ground, its paved streets white ribbons with bugs crawling on them. Fields dotted with patches of mesquite, the airdrome a tiny square seeming to be within a stone's throw of the town, really four miles away.

At four thousand feet he was directly over the field, and started banking more and more steeply to get the feel of the ship. He did figure eights, stalled it, wingturned. And with each moment his touch grew more sure, his heart lighter. That gnawing doubt about his ability vanished slowly but surely.

Suddenly he looked north, and it was a shock to see another D.H. curving toward him. It was Dumpy Scarth and Jack Lee, he thought. The ship came around, diving slightly for his tail. In a moment it had taken position, fifty feet behind and slightly above him.

"He wants a dogfight!" Moran thought. Well, he wouldn't get it. He, Moran, didn't know enough about D.H.s yet—

"? if I'll funk it!" he told himself savagely. "Even if he does show me up."

Mock combat was a favorite diversion—good practise. The point was to get behind and above one's opponent, on his tail, and stay there.

Moran threw his ship into a diving bank, whipping it around heavily. He twisted and turned in wild abandon. He was high enough to be safe. Diving, zooming, going into vertical banks, he tried everything he dared, but Dumpy rode his tail serenely.

It became almost a battle in Moran's mind. ?, how he'd like to show up that little ?, and he couldn't even shake Dumpy off, much less get position himself. Down below he caught a brief glimpse of mechanics and officers watching, and suddenly his heavy jaw set. He'd shake Dumpy off, anyhow, D.H. or no D.H.

And he went into a dive, motor full on. Let Dumpy follow him now, if he was so smart. Those fellows below would find out what kind of a nerve their new flyer had.

The struts were shaking in their sockets, and the wires were screaming with the speed as the motor's roar rose to a veritable bellow.

The airspeed went up slowly—a hundred and seventy, a hundred and ninety, two hundred—

Every instant he was going to pull it out, but with a sort of ferocious joy he held his ship in the dive, second after second. He was hunched deeply into the cockpit, his eyes on his instruments. He'd come down fifteen hundred feet. Now, if Dimpy was on his tail, he'd give up.

He looked around as he started to pull out, using both hands. It was all he could do to move the stick backward. Slowly the ship started to level, vibrating in every spar and strut. Dumpy was nowhere to be seen. He hadn't dared to follow.

The ship was just leveling off, finishing its swoop out, when Moran stiffened. Suddenly the stick seemed to have gone limp in his hands. It came all the way back without resistance.

He had cut the motor to pull out of the dive, and in a panic he shoved the throttle all the way on again. For a moment the ship had wavered, but now it resumed its gradual leveling process. As it came level the nose started to go up into a stall, and Moran, his heart feeling as if it were encased in ice, shoved the stick forward.

The ship did not answer.

He eased the throttle back, and the nose settled. Slowly the frantic pilot looked around. The cabane struts, on the elevators, to which the control wires from the stick were attached, were both leaning toward him. The terrific strain of pulling out of that dive had pulled them loose, and his elevators were useless. He could neither dive nor climb his ship. If he flew until the gas gave out and the propeller stopped, the ship would go into a nose dive which would not end until it hit the ground.

Suddenly Moran's brain seemed preternaturally clear and cool. The fact that sure death apparently awaited him was in the background, merely, of his consciousness, as he methodically thought things out.

The motor was his only hope. The ship seemed perfectly rigged, meaning that at a certain motor-speed it would fly level without the use of stick or rudder. It was flying level now, at fifteen fifty r.p.m. If he cut down the speed of the propeller, it would start diving. The point was that if he sent it into a dive, could he pull it out by turning on full power? Or would the weight of that thousand-pound motor hold it in the dive?

There was but one way to find out. Funny, how little he really felt as his steady hand eased the throttle back to twelve hundred. He seemed to be experimenting for some one else, to be off in another ship, watching a man fight for life.

The nose dropped slowly below the horizon, and he shot the throttle all the way forward. For an agonized moment the D.H. remained in an ever-steepening dive. Then, ever so slowly, the nose came up, and he brought the throttle back slowly to fifteen-fifty.

A chance to wreck, now, in a way that might not kill him. His ailerons and rudders were all right. He sent the ship into a shallow bank, speeding up the motor a trifle to offset the loss of lifting surface, and then straightened it out and headed north. The field adjoining the airdrome north of the fence was rough, but unwooded, and at least three hundred yards long. Then another fence, and a cultivated field. North of this last clearing was mesquite.

Ten miles north of the field he turned again, and headed for the airdrome. He brought the throttle back to fourteen hundred. In a gradual dive the ship sped downward, the airspeed meter crawling up to a hundred and fifty miles an hour. At five hundred feet he was still four miles north of that first cultivated field. Now he brought the throttle back further, and the dive steepened. He let it go for a while— he was about three hundred feet high now—and then shoved it all the way on.

He waited like a statue. Would it level off in time? Two hundred feet, a hundred and fifty, and then the nose started up. The ship was level, a mile back of that first field, and a hundred feet high. Again the throttle crawled back to fourteen hundred. His face was covered with sweat, his feet jumping on the rudder bar. In a series of brief steps he brought it down, and when he leveled the last time his heart leaped as the undercarriage brushed the mesquite. The ship darted across it, and as it cleared it he again inched the gun backward. The dive was so gradual this time that leveling off was almost as easy as doing it with the elevators. The stabilizer was already back, the tail as heavy as it could be made. Three feet above the ground he was rushing along level.

He crashed through the first fence, and the airdrome was close ahead. A wild rush across the intervening field, and the D.H. went through the boundary fence like a cannon ball through paper. He snapped the switches off, and the roar of the motor gave way to the singing of the wires.

He had been going more than a hundred miles an hour. A second after the motor died, the nose dropped suddenly. The D.H. bounced twenty feet in the air. For a second it hovered, stalled, and then crashed as its nose fell.

Moran threw his hands in front of his head. A terrific jar, the splintering of wood and rending of linen. For a second all was blank, and then he found himself tearing his way out of the debris as the odor of burning gasoline assailed his nostrils. Bloody, dazed, only half conscious, he was running, thirty feet from the crackup, as a mass of flame burst from the wreckage, and died into a huge bonfire.

He slowed to a walk, and reason returned to him. Men were rushing from everywhere. Captain Kennard was in the lead, two other flyers behind him.

Moran stopped, his knees wobbly in the reaction. There was but one thought in his mind. He had proved himself a flyer worthy of his trust.

"What happened?"

His eyes met the captain's. The men were fighting the fire, but the officers were gathered about him, Dumpy Scarth in the front.

Moran gathered himself together, and essayed a grin.

"Elevators went wrong on me, that's all," he said with elaborate carelessness. "Brought her down with the motor. Wasn't that a ? of a note?"

The overwrought C.O. went into eruption—

"You're ? right it was a ? of a note! Think you're smart because you got out by a miracle, do you? You're a De Haviland stunt man, are you? What the ? do you mean, diving a D.H. like you did up there, against my orders and against good sense? By ? I don't care whether you kill yourself or not, but ships are ? valuable down here!

"Wipe that sickly grin off your face, ? you! You're entirely too smart for the border, and I don't give a hoot how good a flyer you are. Get that? You're confined to the post for a month, and if the boys weren't flying themselves to death I'd ground you besides. Just as quick as the ?'ll let me I'm going to get you transferred and swap you for somebody I can use."

The doughty captain whirled on Scarth. As if in a dream Moran heard him say savagely:

"As for you, Dumpy, the same thing goes. This is no time for your grandstanding, either. Couldn't resist raising ? with a new man, eh? What do you know about his flying, or what might have happened up there? You save your flying for patrol, understand, and mind your own business in the air and on the ground!"

Scarth flushed, and his mouth opened, but one look into the C.O.'s steely eyes was enough. Kennard took a last shot at Moran.

"A few crashes mean nothing to you, eh? Well, they mean something to me, right now. Hard-boiled egg, are you? Well, I've got no time to take that out of you down here. You'll have a chance to alibi your transfer in just about a week!"

Moran stood there, for a moment, like a dumbly suffering dog. Then, abruptly, curtains seemed to close over his eyes. They were muddy and opaque as he saluted stiffly, and stumbled blindly toward his tent.

He was to be transferred. The subconscious admission that his arraignment had been justified made matters no better. Dumpy Scarth again—

He lay on his cot, forgetting to go to lunch, and gradually his aching misery gave rise to unreasoning hatred for the cocky little flyer who had been his Nemesis.

As the taut days passed, the feeling grew in strength. He was utterly alone, brooding in his tent when he was not forced to appear in public. Dumpy, the irrepressible, had been hurt by his public tonguelashing, too, and he lost no opportunity to razz the black-browed Moran on his landings, which were still far from perfect. Moran rarely answered the taunts of the younger man, but often his eyes were not good to see.

He flew regular patrols, each one a nightmare. That they would soon cease, for him, was only part of the reason. Since that unforgettable landing he had lost all confidence in the De Havilands. A vibrating wire, or a momentary miss in the motor, caused by an air bump, made him tense and uncertain. He was afraid of those big ships which he could not control, as yet, and the memory of his escape from fire awakened him nights, his body covered with sweat and his brain numb.

The occasional efforts of some of the flyers to be sociable, he met with brush rebuffs, and they soon ceased. Every man of them was laboring under a strain. Five, sometimes six, hours of nerve-racking flying each day was their portion, and the waiting for something to break along the Border put the finishing touches on their overwrought condition. Moran, a veritable skeleton at the feast, was relegated to the role of "sorehead," and he knew it. He knew, also, that he was deliberately making his own lot harder, and perversely increasing his own unpopularity as he waited for the ax to fall.

It was not in him, however, to do anything but suffer by himself, and no torture could have dragged a word of admission from him. He lived through the days in dogged silence, masking his bruised spirit behind an impregnable armor of hard self-sufficiency.

It was just before dawn of the fifth day following his wreck that he awakened to find the light on in his tent and Captain Kennard shaking him by the shoulder.

"Listen, Moran," Kennard barked rapidly. "We just got a call, and I'm taking five ships down toward Laralia. Big gang reported coming over the river an hour ago. I'm leaving you and Dumpy Scarth here and taking all the others. Patrol in turn, one of you at the phone all the time. Get up—we're taking off, pronto!"

Moran shivered as he dressed. A norther had been brewing for twenty-four hours, and now the wind was strong and chill. The Libertys were roaring on the line like gargantuan hounds on trail, and dark clouds were scudding across the graying sky. The helmeted flyers were like hooded demons of the night as they got into the cockpits and the ships left the ground in single file, gathering above the field at a thousand feet and hurtling eastward in V-formation like a flock of geese.

Naturally, they'd leave him behind, if anybody, Moran reflected bitterly. Dumpy Scarth had raved because he couldn't go. Moran tried to scotch the ugly knowledge which was in the back of his head. He was not glad that he hadn't been called on to take off in the dank darkness, and fly formation down the border. He was not afraid of De Havilands—

But he knew he was.

The dark, cold day dragged to a close. Three times he went out on patrol, alone, fighting the rising wind every mile of the way and returning to the field a nervous wreck. Some times the ship was thrown about like a leaf, and the tight-lipped, pale Moran lived eternities above the mesquite which seemed reaching upward to drag him down to destruction. The landings were nightmares, in that wind, but he got down safely each time.

He and Dumpy did not speak to each other. When one landed, the other took off. There was no word from the other ships until seven o'clock, as the quick darkness was falling. They had rounded up their prey, but reports of the ground men were that it probably had been false alarm. A bunch of Mexican vaqueros, riding north after some cattle. The ships would stay at Brownsville rather than fight the gale and the darkness combined.

Dumpy returned from his last patrol us the call came in.

"Want the first watch tonight, or the last?" he inquired briefly.

"Either one," Moran told him sullenly.

He was ready to drop. The strain of the day had nearly broken him.

"Then I'll hit the hay. Wake me at twelve," Dumpy told him tersely. Then, characteristically, "Congratulations on the miracle."

Moran looked up quickly to meet the snapping eyes of the younger man.

"Just what do you mean?" he snapped. "What miracle?"

"?, you got down safe, didn't you?" inquired Scarth, with elaborate sarcasm.

Moran's eyes seemed to thicken, and there were red spots in them as he rose to his feet. He bent over, like some heavy-shouldered bear, resting his ham-like hands on the desk as he glared into Dumpy's face. He felt as if he was about to explode—every nerve was raw and jumping. His words were blurred, seeming to come from his lips with difficulty us he mumbled—

"Scarth, I swear that if you don't quit shooting off your mouth—"

"What?" Scarth shot back, perverse enmity in every line of his fat face.

Moran straightened, and his fingers were moving jerkily, his fists closed.

"That I'll ram your teeth down your throat, ? you. Now you get the ? out of here before I throw you out—and don't let me get started on you, do you hear? You've picked on me from the start, and I'll put you in a hospital if you say another ? word!"

Hate was in the air. The indomitable Scarth held his ground, for the moment, before the dark, grim giant whose face reflected black fury and tortured, helpless wrath.

For a long moment their eyes cocked. Suddenly it seemed that Dumpy realized that Moran could have picked him up and broken him in two, and was about to do it. There was a semi-madness in the bigger man's gaze, the fruit of strained days and sleepless nights.

Dumpy's eyes dropped, and he turned toward the door.

"? foolishness to stay at the phone at that," he mumbled uncertainly. "Wind's getting worse every minute. Nobody could go anywhere if they had to."

He went out, and Shag settled down into the chair in front of the desk. The tiny office seemed hardly large enough to contain his huge body. His dull eyes looked into space, and time was non-existent. He had reached the point of physical and mental exhaustion where life itself was merely a bad dream.

He hardly realized that three hours had passed when the shrill of the telephone cut through the howl of the wind. He was a bundle of nerves as he answered its summons.

"Yeah, McMullen flight. Moran. Lieutenant Moran! What the ? does that matter? Kennard's not here. Who? Crosby? Yeah, go ahead."

For a moment he listened to the barked sentences coming out of the night. Automatically his mind registered the facts.

Then:

"We'll see. Try to. 'By."

He rushed to the door, and out into the darkness. The clouds had broken, but fleets of them hurried across the sky, periodically blotting out the moon. The wind came in great gusts, alternating between comparative quiet and the proportions of a gale. As stark fear gripped him he fought it down, cursing himself for a yellow dog as he ran for Dumpy's tent.

The fat little flyer was writing a letter. He looked up in startled surprize as Moran burst into the tent.

"Ever hear of a customs man named Crosby?" Moran rasped.

"Sure. I know him."

"Is there a stool pigeon named José down at Carana—"

"Yes. Keeps the store. We've had trouble before, there. Little Mexican settlement—"

"Crosby just called up and said he landed in Carana and that there's a big bunch of aliens due over within an hour. It'll take a couple of hours before he can get help. Wants us——"

"To fly down!" shouted Scarth, leaping to his feet. "It can't be done! Listen to that wind."

Moran's eyes glittered suddenly.

"He says there's a field down there we've landed in before——"

"Sure there is. But we can't go. Are you crazy? I——"

Moran's contempt for Scarth, his utter contempt for his own yellowness, the fact that life was a hateful thing, all combined to force the words from his lips:

"We could make it. It's our business to. Scared, are you? The famous Dumpy Scarth, who can do so much showing off when there's somebody watching, is scared to death when the real pinch comes, huh? A ? good fair-weather pilot, eh?"

Scarth's curiously boyish eyes gleamed, and his face was white.

"It's—it's suicide, I tell you! At night, this wind——"

"All right, stay here and write your letters!"

Moran stopped at the door, his smouldering eyes playing over the tense, uncertain Scarth. And his tongue flayed the youngster mercilessly as he dared him to come on, until the beleaguered Scarth, his own eyes ablaze, shouted:

"All right. ? you! I can go anywhere you can!"

A moment later stunned mechanics were warming up the ships in the flooding illumination of the huge landing lights, set on top of the hangars. Moran got into his cockpit in a daze, and was the first to taxi out. Mechanics stayed at each wingtip to help him in the wind. Certain that he was going to his death, and scarcely caring, he gave the motor the gun, and fought his ship into the air.

It seemed barely moving against the wind as he cleared the buildings. When be banked to make his turn, the wind almost turned him over, and the D.H. was blown a hundred yards, tipped up steeply, before he could force it level again. Crabbing into the wind, the ship pointed southwest as it flew due west, he looked around for Dumpy.

The other flyer was two hundred yards back of him. Shag, tight-lipped and tense, turned his eyes ahead. The earth was like a shadowed sea, turning from silver-green to black as the clouds continuously blotted out the moon.

The wind caught the ton-and-a-half bomber and played with it exultantly. Often it took all his strength on the stick to hold it level. It shot up and down in the scrambled air currents like a dried leaf in an autumn gale. Should the motor cut out, there was nothing but maiming or death in store for him below. He was breathless and physically sick under the strain. He really expected the ship to go to pieces at any moment, but he fought his way westward doggedly.

It was only a thirty minute flight to Carana, but it took an eternity of time. Twenty miles out the wind seemed to rise, shrieking its resentment at the puny mortals who were defying it. The D.H. was like an outlaw bronco, bucking and pitching in a mad effort to throw its rider. Moran, heavy jaw out-thrust, was suddenly aware of a sort of ferocious joy in fighting it. A lone rider of the storm, he yelled a blasphemous challenge which he could not hear himself, above the devil's song of motor and wind and screaming wires.

Carana, a small collection of lights on the bank of the river, lay ahead only two miles. Dumpy was a mile south, the flames from his motor's exhaust pipes like two fiery red tongues. Moran was looking for Crosby's flashlight signal. Three flashes, and the alien runners were over; four, they were on their way; five, no action as yet and to land on the field, which Dumpy knew, but which Moran did not.

Dumpy was diving for the river now, and Moran, flying in a dream, turned south into the teeth of the storm and labored toward the Rio Grande. Had Scarth seen something below? If he had, it was the job of one ship, at least, to hold the smugglers with its machine guns.

The other one would land, conserving its gasoline supply for the time when the first ship ran low on fuel.

Dumpy was low over the river, a mile west of the settlement. Lights were winking on as Moran, five hundred feet high, looked down at Scarth's ship. The full moon had emerged temporarily from the clouds, and Moran saw what was happening as clearly as if it had been noonday.

Dumpy's ship seemed to stand still in the air, for a moment, as a tremendous gust of wind threw Moran's own plane on its side. As if slapped by the hand of some invisible giant, the left wing of Scarth's D.H. flipped high in the air.

Half on its back, the lower ship plunged into the river in a short upside down dive, and a shower of spray hid it momentarily from the stunned Moran's straining eyes.

It came into view as the water fell. It floated, apparently, in tragic quiet, the motor submerged and the tail high in the air.

Automatically Moran shoved the stick forward. There was no movement below—not an extra ripple on the smooth, turgid water of the river. Dumpy had been knocked out and was helpless beneath the water.

At that second, something within Moran seemed to break. Each taut nerve snapped, and the reaction left him quiet, almost weak, but with his mind clear. He was like a man who has just awakened from a nightmare into reality still more horrible. So much so that the climax of terror left him calm, fatalistic, hopeless.

Motor full on, he sent the frail D.H. hurtling downward in a power dive which made the wires shrill madly and the ship tremble from nose to tail. He was without fear, and his hand was steady as a rock on the stick.

In that brief moment, with the roar of the overspeeding motor dinning in his ears and the peril of the storm surrounding him, he kept his eyes on that wreck below, and saw himself for what he was. He realized what he had done when he had forced Dumpy into this mad trip.

He was calling himself a murderer as he leveled his ship above the water. He was a hundred feet back of that sinister mass, floating so peacefully. He was possessed of a great calm, and he handled his great ship with a sureness he had never known before.

He cut the throttle, and nosed the D.H. upward. It lost speed, and as the stalling point came he threw it into a steep bank, left wing down. He jammed on right rudder at the instant when flying speed was about to disappear, and the De Haviland shot downward on one wing, with scarcely a mile of forward speed.

He gathered himself as the water rushed up to meet him and the airblast flayed his left cheek. The left wing cut the water five feet from Scarth's wreck. The motor plowed into the river, and the ship flipped over, half on its back, as the left wingtip smashed into the bottom of the shallow stream and the entire structure of linen and wood crumpled in a series of ripping, tearing reports.

He was unhurt, and he had unsnapped his belt buckle at the instant of crashing. He was out, wading through the water, which was to his armpits. He took a long breath, and plunged under the other ship.

His groping hands found the body, hanging limply, head downward. His lungs bursting, he heaved upward on the unconscious Scarth, to keep the weight from the belt, and tore at the buckle. It was an eternity before it unfastened, and as he got Scarth above the water he fell limply against the soaked fuselage.

For a moment he had to stay there until his laboring lungs and bursting head grew more normal. Then he stumbled through the water toward the shore. He had scarcely laid Dumpy down when three riders came galloping madly through the mesquite along the river bank.

It was Crosby, with two Mexicans. The customs man took in the situation at a glance, and went to work on the unconscious Scarth with no comment other than a curt:

"If anybody was comin' across tonight they won't now. They'll have heard the ships."

The crude first-aid methods did their work, and Dumpy revived. When his nausea was over Crosby put him on his horse.

"José here can give you a bed to dry out in," the customs man told him cheerily. "Here, Moran, get on José's pony. We'll walk alongside."

As they started slowly up the trail alongside the river Moran ranged his pony alongside Scarth's. There was a great peace within him.

"Scarth," he said slowly, "I was a ? fool tonight. We had no business trying to fly and I—just horsed you into it because we hated each other, I guess. I—"

"'T'sall right," Dumpy mumbled awkwardly. "I was a bigger fool than you. I didn't have to come. And—thanks for pulling me out."

But Moran would not be headed off. He felt that he had to talk, to explain himself to someone.

"I wasn't myself," he went on doggedly. "I got kind of scared of these D.H.s in that wreck, and I was so yellow I just had to fly. I was so scared I wasn't scared, if you get me. I never flew D.H.s before, but razzing you into pretty near a sure accident was—"

"Huh?" grunted Dumpy, his eyes probing Moran's with a curious glitter in them. "You never flew D.H.s before you came down here, you mean?"

Moran nodded.

"I hated to admit it—I wanted to stay, and so I lied and bluffed. I'm just telling you this so that you'll know I wasn't—I didn't mean all that stuff. I was just cuckoo, between one thing and another."

"Well I'll be ?," Dumpy repeated softly, as if musing to himself. He shivered, and seemed to rouse himself from reveries.

"It's all right. Couple o' things got under my hide too, I guess."

"Thanks. Just wanted to—sort of let bygones be bygones before I leave. That'll be in a day or two, I guess."

They relapsed into silence. Moran's face was serious and composed. He did not notice the continuous looks which the impulsive younger man threw at him. He was wrapped in his thoughts. He had burned his bridges behind him in admitting his amateurishness as a flyer, he knew, and any lingering hope that he might stay on the Border was gone. Nevertheless, the bitterness had been purged from him, and he was glad.

At McMullen the next afternoon Dumpy, who had been very thoughtful all day, was first to report to Kennard. Moran changed his clothes, and went to headquarters later. The little captain had one dusty boot on the desk, and he cocked a keen, gray eye at Moran, while he dragged on a cigaret.

"I learned all I had to know from Dumpy," he stated in his husky voice. "Still breaking up my ships, huh?"

Moran's lips widened a trifle in reponse to the twinkle in the C.O.'s eyes.

"So you tried to put across a bluff down here, eh? What a ? fool you are! Well, I'll tell you, Moran. I sometimes like guts more than experience, and I guess if you want to stick around the Border that much, we can stand it. You can get experience here."

Moran's dry mouth opened, but no words came as he saluted and walked out into the flooding sunshine which had followed the storm.

Transcriber's Note: This story appeared in the August 1, 1927 issue of Adventure magazine.